OHOMAN AND THE SPIRITS OF THE MOUNTAIN

By

Gerald M. Reiche

Gabriel—

Remember that dreams are only dreams until you start walking the path to make them a reality.

Gerald M. Reiche
11-19-06

ISBN: 1-4033-0293-6 (Electronic)
ISBN: 1-4033-0294-4 (Softcover)
ISBN: 1-4033-0295-2 (Hardcover)

This book is printed on acid free paper.

1st Books – rev 05/29/02

OHOMAN AND THE
SPIRITS OF THE MOUNTAIN

WRITTEN BY GERALD M REICHE

ILLUSTRATED BY DAVID DUDT

ILLUSTRATED BY DAVID DUDT

Dedication

This book is dedicated to my family
For their loving support and encouragement
In the following of my dream

TABLE OF CONTENTS

CHAPTER	PAGE

TABLE OF ILLUSTRATIONS

CHAPTER 1

A GRATEFUL PEOPLE

Long ago when buffalo covered the land and the world was full of life there lived a gentle people called the Moralites.

For many years they lived peacefully in a big valley. Next to their valley were mountains that were so tall that they touched the sky.

The earth inside their valley was dark and rich. Plants grew so thick and tall that the Moralites never had to worry about having enough food.

Between the dark, rich valley and the tall mountains was a thick forest of ancient trees that provided homes for many wild animals. The Moralites sometimes went into the forest and gathered long sturdy branches that had fallen from the trees. They used them to build their homes and corrals for their horses.

There was a river of cool, fresh water that made its way from the snow at the top of the mountains, down through the forest and across their valley. It provided them with an endless supply of fish and water.

A Land Rich and Beautiful

Gerald M. Reiche

The Moralites were very grateful for all the things that the Earth gave them. They showed their thanks by learning to respect and live in harmony with the world around them. They made costumes and sang songs and danced in celebration of the good things that were part of their lives. Some songs told stories about their ancestors. Some dances told stories about where the Moralites came from. Other songs and dances told about the importance of the Earth and the animals that lived there. But their favorite was the story of "Ohoman and the Spirits of the Mountain". It reminded them of the choices that their ancestors made and how those choices led them to this valley by the great mountains.

Gerald M. Reiche

Giving Thanks for Life

Gerald M. Reiche

The stories were always told by the Ancients. They were the Elders of the tribe. They were chosen to pass down the history of their people because they had lived through so much of it themselves. Not the entire Moralite history, mind you, but more than any of the others in the tribe.

The children looked forward to hearing the Ancients speak. Their stories were colorful and full of adventure. So, every morning while the men went to hunt for that day's supper; while the women went about their daily activities, the children gathered inside the circle of the Ancients to hear the stories of their people.

Awanay was the eldest of the Ancients. No one knew how old he was. Awanay himself had stopped counting the seasons a long time before. All they knew was that he had been there as long as anyone could remember. Some even believed that he was one of the first Moralites.

Gerald M. Reiche

The Ancient Awanay

Gerald M. Reiche

The children often asked Awanay if this was true. But Awanay would only raise his hands to quiet them and begin his story. Being the eldest, it was his place to tell the story that held the greatest meaning to his people. And so, they would hear of Ohoman.

Awanay was an incredible storyteller. His words came forth like music from the heavens. His hands, wrinkled with age, moved smoothly across the sky, giving life to the years that had passed so long before. But the most amazing things to the children were Awanay's eyes. They were a rich, dark brown that carried the light of a thousand seasons. Those who caught their gaze were filled with a warmth that instantly told them of the greatness that was held inside. A closer look into them brought a clarity of mind that was like the opening of a window. And the more they looked, the more the window opened until it was no more. They had become part of it. Part of the greatest story of their people.

CHAPTER 2

THE BIRTH OF A LEGEND

The story began with the birth of a young warrior named "Ohoman". His name meant, "One Who Is Strong And Full Of Life." He was named after a beautiful, white stallion that roamed the mountains.

For many years the Moralite warriors had tried to catch the stallion, but he always proved too strong and swift for them. Too swift even for Hetamet. But then Hetamet had known this from the first time that he set eyes on the stallion. "This one" he would say "will never be caught."

Hetamet was the greatest warrior that the Moralites had ever known. Tall, strong, fleet of foot, yet compassionate and wise. Everyone looked to him for guidance, even the Elders. But it was not just because he was strong and wise, it was because he used his strength and wisdom to help his people in their greatest time of need.

The Great Hetamet

Gerald M. Reiche

It had only been three winters, but already it was spoken of as one of the greatest legends of their people. It was during the worst winter that they had ever experienced. The snowfall started early that season. So early that none knew if they had stored enough food to last until spring. As the winter progressed, the snow fell harder and harder with fewer and fewer days between storms. This made it impossible to hunt. Soon it became clear that there would not be enough food to last. But the snow had become so deep that neither the braves nor their ponies could go very far without help. And still the snow came down.

It was not long before the people became hungry and sick. But each time one of the braves ventured out to search for food, the storms raged and sent them back, empty handed.

Things were becoming desperate. Then, Hetamet went out and gathered the strongest of the braves. He had seen them each try to go out on their own only to fail. He told them that if they went out together they would surely do better. So they all went out into the snow together.

One by one, they took their turns paving the way for the others. It was hard, but Hetamet was right. They were going farther than any one man had gone before. But they had not won the battle just yet. The snow began falling harder than ever. It was as if someone was covering their tracks with a blanket. Soon it became difficult to see.

Hetaet told the others that if they could not see the village and if the snow covered their trail, they might not find their way back. So they traveled as far as they could without losing sight of the village. One brave was then chosen to stay so that the rest could be guided back on their return. But the forest was still far away and the snow continued to fall. They decided that they would leave a brave behind each time they reached the edge of their sight of the brave that was left before. They did this until they reached the forest.

When they finally did reach the forest, there was only Hetamet. All of the others were part of the human trail that would lead them back to their people. But how long could they last outside in the elements? Hetamet did not want to find out. He needed to move quickly to find food and return.

Immediately Hetamet chose his plan of action. He would go to those parts of the forest where he had always found game before.

It seemed like hours had passed by the time he arrived at the first clearing. But he did not find the game that was always so plentiful there. He moved on to the next place, and the next, and the next. But there was no game. No food to bring home to his people. But he could not give up.

Finally Hetamet arrived at the last, the farthest hunting ground. He was exhausted from his battle with the high drifts of snow. It had been a long, hard journey but he was sure he would find game. But, again there was nothing.

Gerald M. Reiche

Hetamet Sees the Great Stallion

Gerald M. Reiche

Sadly, Hetamet looked down. He thought about his people. For the first time in his life he felt he was going to fail them. But the sadness quickly turned into determination. Looking at the snow that fell around him, he took his hand, raised it high into the air and clenched it into a fist. He began shouting at the sky, then at the forest around him. "Take me if you must but you will not take my people!" His voice echoed a thunderous tone that seemed to carry on for miles. That is when it happened.

Now, some say that it was the power of his spirit that caused the snow to stop; that it was his will for his people that caused the animals to come forth. Still, others say that the Great Spirit heard Hetamet's cry that day; that Hetamet had shown such love for his people that It sent a beautiful white stallion as a message. They say it was the stallion's voice that silenced the sky. It was the stallion's call that brought forth the animals. It was the stallion's trail that led Hetamet back to his people. No one really knows exactly. Not even Hetamet could say for sure. But it was the first time Hetamet saw the stallion. It was a beautiful animal with a spirit like no other he had ever seen. It truly was a gift from the Spirits. One that would never be tamed. It was not meant to be. That is how Hetamet knew that it could not be caught.

The next three years proved to be very good to the Moralites. The weather was kind and the food plentiful. Even Hetamet enjoyed the good fortune that had been bestowed upon his people.

The year following the snow, Hetamet married. It was not long after that Hetamet found himself pacing outside the communal hut, waiting for the village midwife to announce the birth of his child. He was sure that there would soon be a small boy that he could show to his people. He would call the boy "Ohoman".

Hetamet saw the stallion close by the village just before Ohoman was born. It was strange for him to stand so close to the village. But when Ohoman cried with his first breath, everyone knew why the stallion was there. They watched as he reared and kicked his feet high into the air. At the same time, the stallion called out as if to say that a great spirit had been born. One that would grow strong and have great wisdom and who would do many wonderful things for his people. Then the stallion ran into the forest.

The Birth of Ohoman

Gerald M. Reiche

The Moralite warriors chased after him as they always did. And, as usual, they came back with stories of how they had nearly caught the great stallion.

But this time there was more to tell! The stallion did not just outrun them. This time he ran into a strange mist, deep in a canyon. Then, as if the Earth had opened up and swallowed him, the stallion disappeared! The Moralite warriors tried to follow the stallion into the canyon, but there was nothing to follow. No sounds of hoofs hitting the ground, no hoofprints in the dirt, nothing. Only the sound of his voice echoing around them.

Hetamet suspected that there was more to the story. When the stallion first appeared, the harsh winter became mild and his people flourished. Since that time, he had seen his people become soft and less concerned with the world around them. Did the disappearance of this beautiful animal signal a change?

CHAPTER 3

OHOMAN BECOMES A MAN

The years after Ohoman's birth passed quickly. His father was very proud of him. He could run farther and faster than any of the other boys. He could move through the thickest brush without making a sound. He could draw and shoot an arrow faster and farther and more accurately than anyone. But even though he was bigger, stronger and more skilled than the others, he was very gentle and kind to everyone. If there was noone to hunt for them, he brought them food. If a boy lost his father, Ohoman would teach the boy how to be a great warrior so he could take care of his family and bring honor to them. These were only some of the things that Ohoman did to help his people.

Ohoman Becomes a Warrior

Gerald M. Reiche

But there was more to Ohoman than just helping others in need. As he grew, he began to understand the relationship between his people and the Earth around them. He understood the importance of living with nature. He understood that all life depends on all other life to survive. These were the laws that his father had taught him.

But not everyone in the village believed in these laws as Ohoman did. There were those who believed that the Spirits had created the Earth for *them*. They believed that the animals were created to provide food and clothing. They believed the forest was created to provide wood for shelter and fuel for campfires. They believed that no matter how much they took from the Earth, there would always be enough. They believed that the Spirits would see to this.

It troubled Ohoman greatly to see so many of his people take so much from the Earth. He tried to warn them of their wastefulness, but they would not listen. Instead they waved their hands across the valley. "Look at all the Spirits have given us!" They would tell him. "You tell us that if we take from the Earth, it will one day be gone. But each year our people go into the forest and bring back more than the year before. Surely you must see that what you say is wrong!"

"Yes," Ohoman would answer, "Each year you take more. But each year you must go deeper into the forest to find game. Each year you must go further upstream to fish. Each year you must clear more trees to find fertile ground for your crops. Do you not see that one day there will be no more? Who will feed your children then?"

CHAPTER 4

THE END OF THE WORLD

More years went by. It was just as Ohoman had described. Each year the people went deeper into the now disappearing forest to hunt the few animals that remained. The fish were fewer and the once rich Earth had become like dust that rose and fell with the wind.

Ohoman helped his people as much as he could. He rode with them in search of food. But what was once an easy task was now a long and sometimes fruitless journey into the mountains. When they found game, Ohoman tried to tell the others to take only what was needed and leave the rest so that maybe one day there would be more. But the others rarely listened. "Look!" They would tell him, "The Spirits have provided for us again. All is well now."

Soon Ohoman began to realize that his people were not going to listen. They had too long lived the life of greed. They had no respect for the delicate balance of nature. They had over hunted and over fished. They no longer cared for their work animals. They no longer sang the songs or danced the dances that thanked the Earth for giving them life.

Ohoman was sad inside. He felt that he had failed in his life as a great warrior. Instead of his people learning to live with the world, he saw them try to rule the world. They thought they were better, wiser than the lowly animals around them. "After all," they would say, "fish cannot talk, deer cannot build houses, and wolves cannot wield a bow and arrow." But inside, Ohoman also knew that there was good in his people. And so he kept trying. Even though they laughed at him. Even though the leaders voted him out of the village, he kept his faith. For he knew that one-day they would listen to him and things would change.

The People Come to Ohoman for Help

Gerald M. Reiche

That one-day did come. It came on a day when the other warriors returned from their hunt with empty hands. They came to see Ohoman that day. They told him that there were no more animals to hunt, that the fish were gone and the plants were dying. Finally they saw what their wastefulness had brought them. Their world was dead.

CHAPTER 5

THE SEARCH FOR LIFE

Knowing that his people would not last much longer, Ohoman left the village to find them another place to live. It had been a long time since anyone had left the village. There were no more horses. They had been sacrificed for the greater good. So now, those who tried to leave for greener pastures could only go as far as their feet could take them. Most returned, saying that there was no place else to go. The land was the same as far as they could see. Those who did not return were presumed to have died in the vast wasteland that they had helped to create.

Ohoman had to leave. There was nothing more he could do for his people there. He did not want to watch them die. So he took what he could carry and began his walk to find a better life for them.

It was a very long walk, filled with much sorrow. Everywhere he looked he saw the destruction that his people had brought to the land. It was hard to believe that it was once lush and full of life.

Finally, after many days, he came to the base of the mountains that formed the edge of his valley. They were tall mountains. He knew that he could climb them, but there was not enough time. The seasons were due to change soon and his people could not endure another winter.

Suddenly, Ohoman saw something that he had not seen for a long time. There was a deer wandering by the side of a large outcropping of rocks. Ohoman could not believe his eyes! He stood, frozen, watching the deer as it explored the ground around it.

"Surely I must be dreaming." He told himself. Then, the deer caught sight of Ohoman and disappeared behind the rocks.

Ohoman decided to see where the deer had gone. He went to the rocks. He did not see the deer, but there were tracks. Ohoman knelt down and placed two of his fingers on one of the hoof prints. Satisfied that he had not imagined it, he followed the tracks. They led to another, smaller outcropping of rocks and stopped. Seeing no other choice, Ohoman began to climb. Then he saw it. Twenty, maybe thirty feet up the side of the mountain, hidden in the shadows, was a cave. At the foot of the cave were more tracks that led inside. Ohoman followed them into the cave. Within minutes, the cave became a dark tunnel. But before he had time to find a wall to guide him, Ohoman saw an opening with sunlight in the distance. In that sunlight, he could make out the figure of the deer. It was looking at him as if waiting for him to follow. He moved quickly toward the opening. But by the time he reached it, the deer was gone.

Ohoman Follows a Deer to a New World

Gerald M. Reiche

Ohoman peered out from the cave into a great valley. Excitedly, he stepped out into the light. He looked around in amazement. Then he cast his sight to the other side of the valley at the mountains that formed its border.

He looked up at the top of the mountains and saw snow that became waterfalls. The waterfalls became a river that gave life to a thick forest. At the edge of the forest was the valley.

He walked to the center of the valley and found a trail that pointed towards the mountains. He followed the trail. Soon he found himself winding through the forest where animals scattered from his path.

Ohoman could not believe all the life that surrounded him! Taking in a great breath, he thought what a wonderful place this would be to bring his people.

Gerald M. Reiche

The Sacred Path

Gerald M. Reiche

.

Ohoman followed the trail for a long time. Soon shadows from the mountains foretold the setting of the sun. He watched for a clearing to stop and set camp. Farther and farther he walked, but there was no clearing. Only thick brush and trees. Looking up, he saw stars begin to twinkle in a darkening sky. He walked faster, hoping that he would find a place soon. Maybe around the next bend in the trail. But the next bend came and went, as did the next, and the next. There was still no clearing. Only the thin trail winding through a lush wall of trees.

Soon the last of the light faded and Ohoman was surrounded by the dark. But he was not afraid. He had spent many nights hunting in the darkness. He had always found his way. But this was a strange place. There was no moon and the trees now blocked even the sparkle of the stars from his view.

The night grew darker and darker. Ohoman could no longer see the trail. He had to stop.

Suddenly, a cold wind blew across his face! It sent chills shooting up and down his body. He pulled a buffalo skin from his bundle and drew it around himself.

Another wind blew! This time it circled him. Then, it stopped.

Ohoman stood silently, waiting to see what would happen next. His muscles tightened as he listened to the darkness. His senses told him that something was near. A bear? A wolf? No. This was something else. Something completely different than he had ever faced before.

Ohoman could feel the blood rushing through his veins as he prepared for battle. He turned around in a slow circle, trying to feel where the attack would be.

Suddenly, he felt something behind him. He spun around, knife in hand, ready to face the beast! But there was no beast. Instead, he saw a strange, ghostly figure floating above his head.

Ohoman stared at the figure for a moment. Then he looked around him. As he did, others appeared. Quickly they surrounded him. Ohoman had fought many battles with many animals. Sometimes he had even fought more than one at a time. But there were too many of these strange creatures. He knew that he could not fight them all and live. So he lowered his hands and let go the knife. He steadied himself against the darkness and watched and waited for what would come next. But the creatures kept their distance.

Ohoman waited. He looked at the creatures around him. They still did not move. It was if they were waiting for him to speak. So he raised himself as tall and proud as he had ever done. He looked once more at them and in a powerful voice called out: "I am Ohoman, strongest and bravest warrior of the Moralites. Who are you and what do you want of me?"

Gerald M. Reiche

The Spirits Appear

Gerald M. Reiche

The creatures did not speak. Instead, they began moving around him. They darted back and forth, up and down. Some passed close to his face. Others near his chest. Ohoman stood silently. After a few minutes, he called out again: "I am Ohoman, strongest and bravest warrior of the Moralites. Who are you and what do you want of me?" This time he did not have to wait long for a reply.

"We are the Spirits of the mountain!" A voice thundered. "Who are you to enter this land!"

Ohoman quickly realized that he was standing on sacred ground. He humbled his voice.

"Please forgive me, kind Spirits. I did not know that this was sacred ground. I have come from far away in search of a home for my people. The land they now call home has died. The crops do not grow and the animals have gone. If I do not find a place for them, they will surely die."

"Then they will die!" The voice thundered again. "We have seen how your people disgrace the Earth. If we let them come they will kill this place as they have killed their own. Leave! Tell them they are not welcome here!"

"No…" Ohoman started to speak. But he could not. Something had grabbed him inside. It seemed to pull the air out of him. He bent over, trying to breathe.

"You are evil! Your people are evil! Be gone!" The Spirit's words echoed through the darkness. Then, all was quiet.

Ohoman finally caught his breath. Standing up, he looked around him. The Spirits were gone. He was alone. But he could not give up. He shouted into the darkness, "I am not evil! I have lived my life as one with the land. The Earth is my mother, the animal my friend! I would not harm them any more than I would harm myself! If you are the great Spirits that you claim to be you know this to be true."

As soon as the words left Ohoman's mouth, one of the Spirits appeared before him. Slowly it rose above him where it began to glow and twist and spin. Ohoman stared at the sight. He watched as it grew and changed forms. First it became a river of white, like a waterfall crashing down from the heavens into a lake below. He felt the wetness of the mist as it spread over him. Then it became a dark, thunderous cloud that shot lightning from its belly. Ohoman watched and listened as light crackled into the darkness. And when the cloud became silent, there appeared an eagle, bright with the glow of fire that flew from its wings as they spread across the sky. It was a sharp contrast to the cool mist of the waterfall.

Ohoman watched the eagle's wings move back and forth across the night. He saw streams of fire shoot from them. For an instant, he became afraid that the fire would engulf him. But it did not. The fire became streaks of light that fell into a circle around him.

Gerald M. Reiche

Ohoman's Vision

Gerald M. Reiche

Ohoman stood, powerless. He looked up. Fire continued to fly from the eagle. Only now, the fire flowed like a river into the darkness, changing to light as it made its way into the circle around him. Back and forth moved the wings, like branches of great trees floating in the wind. He could feel the heat burning into his skin. Faster and faster the wings moved. Taller and taller grew the circle around him.

Ohoman looked around him. He could see nothing but the light. He looked up. The light had grown into a high, spinning tunnel that seemed to go on forever. Then, his ears caught the sound of a low, mournful cry. He looked around to see where the sound was coming from, but saw only the light. His eyes squinted as he tried to pierce through the light. But they could not. Again his ears caught the sound. It was closer this time. But he still could not see.

Suddenly Ohoman realized that the sound was not coming from outside the light, but from the light itself! The Spirits were crying out to him!

Ohoman stood silently. He closed his eyes and focused on the sound that now surrounded him. It was a sad, lonely sound. It reminded him of the howl of a mother wolf that came back to her den to find that her young had been taken from her.

The weeping grew louder. Pictures of buffalo herds filled his mind. He could hear their cries as one after another of them fell from the shot of an arrow. But few of the dead were taken for food. Even fewer for the warmth of their hides.

Ohoman continued to listen to the howling of the Spirits. Pictures continued to run through his mind of the lives wasted by the greed of a once great people. Their cries grew louder. The pictures ran faster and more numerous than Ohoman could see. Louder and louder, faster and faster. Soon they became like one, long scream.

Ohoman could take no more. He covered his ears to try and shut the Spirits out. But he could not. They were in his mind, shrieking their lament to him. He fell to his knees, screaming for them to stop his torment. But they did not stop. Instead, the screaming became louder and louder until he felt as if it would burst from his very being!

Then, suddenly, all was quiet.

Ohoman was relieved. He took in a long breath. He opened his eyes and looked around him. He waited to see what would happen next. But nothing happened. There was only the quiet, the darkness and the pounding of his heart.

CHAPTER 6

THE SECRET OF THE MOUNTAIN

Ohoman sat quietly. He breathed deep and calmed his heart. After what seemed like an eternity, one of the Spirits appeared and came close to him. Ohoman stood quickly and faced toward it.

The Spirit came closer and closer. Ohoman remained steadfast. He watched as the Spirit touched against him. It remained there only for an instant, then vanished.

Another eternity passed until the Spirit appeared before him again.

"Ohoman," the Spirit spoke gently to him, "we have looked into your heart. We know you are a great and kind warrior with the wisdom of the Elders. We believe that you speak the truth. Your search to save your people is an honorable one; one that deserves our respect. And so it shall be that you shall learn the secret of this place. Watch. Listen."

Ohoman watched as the Spirit rose high above him again. He saw the spirit begin to glow and twist and spin into the shape of a small, white cloud. Then the cloud grew until it covered the sky. Then the Spirit spoke.

"Many years ago, people lived on this land. They were a gentle people. They lived here in peace with each other, the Earth and the animals. They understood the importance of treating the Earth with respect. They knew that all life depends on all other life to survive."

"These people honored their Mothers and Fathers. They also honored the animals which served them in life. When the Great Spirit of Death came to their homes, their bodies were taken across the river to rest at the base of the great mountains. This pleased us. So we vowed to keep watch over them so long as they lived on this land. And so it was for many generations. The path where you now stand was their sacred path to that place."

Gerald M. Reiche

The Secret of the Mountain

Gerald M. Reiche

"One day, a boy was born who never learned the old ways. He did not understand that a seed could not grow if it was not planted; and so it was for everything. But because his people had been so good to the Earth for so long, because there was more than enough, his people did not see the effect the boy had on the Earth around them until it was too late."

"As the years passed, this young boy became the leader of his people. They followed him as he over fished and over hunted. This angered us so we drove the people far away from this land. Far away from the valley and the great mountains."

Suddenly Ohoman felt ashamed for his people. He looked away from the Spirit.

"Why do you look away?" asked the Spirit. "Why do things that happened so long ago shame you now?"

"Great Spirit," Ohoman said, "I know that my people have dishonored the Earth. I know that this is why you have spoken to me in this way. But I also know that they are a good people. Please give them the chance to show that they are worthy of this land and your protection."

But the Spirit did not answer. Ohoman looked up to plead with the Spirit, but it was gone.

For the first time in Ohoman's life, he felt helpless. He felt that he had failed his people by not trying harder to teach them the old ways. Kneeling down he lowered his head to ponder the words of the Spirit, and his promise to his people.

CHAPTER 7

A NEW BEGINNING

Ohoman knelt quietly for a long time. He could not help thinking about what the Spirit had said. He wondered if they were going to give his people a chance.

Images of his people flashed in his mind. He saw them in their huts. The children were crying because they had no food. He saw his people's burial ground. He thought how much it had grown in recent years.

Suddenly he heard something in the distance. Ohoman cleared his mind and listened. The sound came again. It was too far away to make out. But there was something familiar about it. Ohoman closed his eyes and waited for the sound. Hearing it once more, he knew what he had to do. He had to go to the mountain!

Ohoman stood up. He looked for the mountain, but the darkness blinded him. "Which way?" he thought to himself. He felt lost. Then he heard the sound again. It was calling to him! He had to get to the mountain!

Slowly he moved forward, feeling his way along the sacred path. Then something pulled at him. He quickened his pace. He felt another tug and moved faster.

Ohoman stumbled and fell. He stood up and moved forward again. He listened for the sound, hoping that it would help guide him through the dark.

Suddenly he felt something take control of his legs. They began to move faster along the trail. Soon he found himself running. Fearful that he might end up at the bottom of a cliff, he tried to slow down. But he could not. His legs were no longer his to control. They kept pumping, moving him forward like wheels on a train. Then, they stopped.

Ohoman waited to see what would happen next. He called to the Spirits, but there was no reply. He called a second time. Still nothing. He closed his eyes. Raising his head, he felt the cool air brush against his face. He could hear the rushing of water in the distance. He knew that he was close to the river, which meant the mountain was not far away.

All at once he felt tired. So tired that it was difficult to open his eyes. He reached for his buffalo skin and pulled it around himself. Then he lay down and slept.

In his sleep he saw a village. In the middle of the village, people were crowded around a hut. They were waiting for something. Behind them, by the edge of the woods, a beautiful, white stallion appeared. The people watched as it reared and kicked its feet high into the air. At the same time it called out to them. Then it disappeared in a strange mist and the cry of a baby took its place.

Ohoman awoke with a start! He had been given his answer! His people would have their chance!

"Thank you, kind Spirits. I will bring my people here. They will show you that they are truly worthy."

No sooner had Ohoman made his promise than he heard a sound. It was the same sound that summoned him to the mountain!

Slowly, Ohoman turned toward the river. He could see the moon starting to rise over the tops of the great mountains. He looked down and across the river and watched as hundreds of Spirits appeared. At the front of them, nearest the water, was the spirit of a beautiful, white stallion, galloping back and forth along the bank of the river. His long mane and tail floated behind him. Ohoman watched as the stallion skid to a halt, reared and pawed at the air. Then, looking straight at Ohoman, the stallion called to him.

Call of the Spirit Stallion

Gerald M. Reiche

CHAPTER 8

THE CHOSEN ONES

Ohoman stared in awe. He had seen this stallion in his dreams a thousand times! It was always the same. Galloping back and forth along the water, rearing up and calling to him. He never understood the dream until now.

Ohoman quickly gathered himself. His Father told him from the day of his birth that he was destined to do great things for his people. Now his time had come.

"We have looked into your heart, Ohoman. You are the chosen one. Bring your people back to the Earth."

Ohoman turned around to thank the Spirits. But there were none. He looked back across the river. All of the Spirits had disappeared except for the stallion which reared once more and called out to him. "This is your destiny, Ohoman. Bring those who believe in the old ways. Bring life back to your people and purpose back to us."

Ohoman returned to his people. Those who believed in the old ways were waiting for him. The others had died from their wastefulness or gone elsewhere in search of a new place to call home. They were not heard from again.

Ohoman told his people about the mountains, the forest and the valley. He told them about the Spirits and of their promise to protect those who believed in the old ways. He told them of the secrets he had learned about the mountains and why the people were driven away. Then he took them to the valley, to the sacred path. There, each was judged by the truth of their own heart.

Since that time the Moralites have remained faithful to the old ways. They respect the Earth, the animals and each other. They dance their dances and sing their songs of thanks for what the Earth has brought them.

They still walk the sacred path to the mountain. And every so often, it is said that one can see the spirit of a proud warrior riding a beautiful, white stallion along the bank of the river.

Gerald M. Reiche

The Spirit of Ohoman

Gerald M. Reiche

How to Order This Book

"Ohoman" is available in three formats: E-Book
and Hard cover and Soft cover.
To order this book as an E-Book, contact 1st Books
Library at www.1stbooks.com

To order this book in hard cover or soft cover
format, please either contact
1st Books Library or check with your localbookstore.

If you would like an autographed copy of
"Ohoman" in book format,
simply fill out the form located below and
mail it to:

OHOMAN
P O Box 0671
Santa Clarita, CA 91380-0671

All autographed copy requests must include
payment for the purchase
price of the book plus $3.00 for postage and
handling.

OHOMAN ORDER FORM

Name_____

Address_____

City_____State_____Zip_____

Telephone_____

Price $_____ea_____Quantity of Hard Cover _____

Price: $_____ea_____ Quantity of Soft Cover _____

Name of person(s) receiving book (if different than above)_____

If you have a specific request other than listed above, please send it C/O Ohoman at the above address.

Please allow 2-4 weeks for delivery.

Gerald M. Reiche

OHOMAN ORDER FORM

Name_____

Address_____

City_____State_____Zip_____

Telephone_____

Price $_____ea_____Quantity of Hard Cover _____

Price: $_____ea_____ Quantity of Soft Cover _____

Name of person(s) receiving book (if different than above)_____

If you have a specific request other than listed above, please send it C/O Ohoman at the above address.

Please allow 2-4 weeks for delivery.

Gerald M. Reiche

About the Illustrator

David Dudt is a native of Colorado with an education in commercial and fine art from the University of Colorado.

As well as selling his works privately, David has also won various competition awards. He is a multi-media artist who incorporates a background of Asian studies, Native American spirituality and a love for Mother Nature in his works.

David currently resides in Palm Springs, California.

FUTURE WORKS

The following is the list of books Mr. Reiche is currently working on as well as their anticipated release dates:

"Images in Time".....................Summer, 2003

A "How To" Book on the
Equestrian Arts (As yet untitled) ...Summer, 2004

"The Constable", a mystery series... Summer, 2005

Other works and titles to be announced.

ABOUT THE AUTHOR

Gerald Miles Reiche was raised in Southern California He carries a BA in English and a Juris Doctor. After years of working in insurance related fields, and with the loving support of his family, Gerald turned to his long time dream of writing.

Gerald's other interests include everything from karate to the equestrian arts. He is a prolific writer, gifted with the ability to weave imagination and fantasy into a realistic world from which the reader finds it difficult to leave.

Gerald hopes that you will enjoy his work and learn from it how incredible a gift of imagination can be.

Printed in the United States
6531